Margie Makes a

Difference

Lady Tigers' Series

By

Dawn Brotherton

Dawn Brotherton (signature)

Margie Makes a Difference

Lady Tigers Series

Published by Blue Dragon Publishing.

www.blue-dragon-publishing.com

Copyright 2017 Dawn Brotherton

ISBN 978-1-939696-14-4 (ePub)

ISBN 978-1-939696-18-2

Library of Congress Control Number: 2017902385

Illustrations and cover by Vineet Siddhartha

http://www.DawnBrothertonAuthor.com

Printed in the U.S.A.

 Blue Dragon Publishing

Dedication

To my daughters who have always been
my biggest fans. Thanks for your
unwavering support and feedback.

Other books by this author:
Lady Tigers' Series

Trish's Team
Margie Makes a Difference
Nicole's New Friend (coming soon)

Softball Scoresheet

Chapter 1

Margie Clark focused as the ball came off the bat and sped towards her position at second base. Keeping her head down as she had been taught, Margie charged the ball, scooping it into her glove. Smoothly, she grabbed it with her right hand and fired the ball to the first baseman.

"Out!" the umpire yelled with an upward movement of his right arm.

A cheer rose from the crowd and the pitcher ran over to give Margie a high five.

From across the field, Margie heard a distinct voice above the others. "Nice play, Pumpkin!"

She looked to see her dad standing along the fence near right field next to her mother.

1

Her heart swelled with pride as she took in the gray-green, camouflage Air Force uniform he wore most days to work. His broad smile gave Margie confidence. She was really glad he was here.

Since June when Margie was selected for the Lady Tigers' fourteen and under travel softball team, she had spent most weekends practicing or at tournaments. The highly competitive team was part of a larger organization that picked the best softball players in the area from ages eight to eighteen. During a weekend tournament, they often played three to four games a day. She had become close to the girls on her team and loved to spend time with them, but having her dad at the game always made the day extra special.

"One more, ladies! Let's go!" Coach Kory Kerrington cheered from the dugout.

Margie tried to stay focused, but she was excited to see her dad. He was a master sergeant in the Air Force and worked on airplanes. He had to work all hours and sometimes go to different bases for weeks at a time. Because of that, he missed a lot of games. He had been gone the last few weeks and must have come straight to the game from his travels.

Margie turned her attention back to the batter. She heard the third baseman yell bunt, but it took a few seconds for it to register. The pitcher and the first baseman were already running toward the ball that the batter had expertly put down only a few feet in front of the plate and on the first base line.

Too late, Margie rushed to beat the batter to first base. The first baseman ran forward, picked up the ball barehanded, and turned to throw the ball to first. Margie was still steps away and missed the perfectly thrown ball as it and the batter crossed the bag. Panic threatened to overwhelm Margie as she realized she had missed an easy out.

She was relieved when she turned to see the right fielder had run in to back up the throw and easily scooped up the ball, holding the batter at first. The right fielder tossed the ball back to the pitcher.

"It's all right, girls," Assistant Coach Sam Elliot said. "Nothing hurt. Get the next one."

Sulking back to her position, Margie was too embarrassed to look up. Taking off her glove, she took time to tighten the rubber band holding the auburn waves out of her face.

"Brush it off," she heard her dad yell. "Never quit!"

Straightening her shoulders and putting her left hand back inside the glove, she nodded slightly. She wasn't going to let it happen again.

Thankfully she didn't have a chance to test her resolve. The pitcher threw three strikes in a row, earning the final out of the game for the Lady Tigers. The girls rushed in to pat her on the back and line up to shake hands with the other team.

"Don't look so glum," Trish Murphy said, giving Margie a playful nudge as they headed to the dugout. "Everyone makes mistakes."

"Not when my dad's watching," she said miserably. She cringed as she realized what she said. Although Trish's dad had been coming to some games, he missed more than he came to. She knew it bothered Trish that her dad played golf most Sundays rather than coming to her games.

Trish shrugged it off. "I know what you mean. Your dad is here, so you want to show off for him. Totally understandable. But don't worry about it. He knows you're great!"

Margie knew she should feel lucky. Her dad came whenever he wasn't working and, with the Air Force, his schedule was unpredictable. She tried to look on the bright side. Some military parents were gone for months at a time—or a whole year!

The girls packed their gear and joined their teammates in the shade under the tree behind the dugout.

Sally Andrews and her sister Nikki moved over for Trish and Margie to flop on the grass beside them.

"Your dad looks awesome in his uniform," Nikki said to Margie.

"I honestly didn't even see him until he cheered," Sally added. "I guess the camouflage really works!" The team giggled at the thought of hiding at a softball field.

The girls were interrupted by the arrival of their three coaches. "Great game, ladies," Coach Kory said. "Once again, you stuck together and didn't get flustered by errors."

Margie felt her face get hot with embarrassment. She ducked her head and let her hair cover her face.

Coach Dave added, "Everyone makes mistakes. It's part of the game. It's how you recover that shows what you're made of. It's only mid-July. We have plenty of softball left this season."

"Coach Sam? Do you have anything to add?" Coach Kory asked the third coach.

"Sticks, sticks, sticks. I'm not sure what you were afraid of those first few innings. Most of you didn't even look like you wanted to swing the bat. If you swing, you at least have a chance. If you keep the bat on your shoulder, there's a one hundred percent chance you won't hit the ball."

The girls hung their heads. They had heard this speech and knew what he said was true. That didn't make getting into the batter's box any less intimidating.

Coach Sam went on, "You finally picked up around the third inning. Tomorrow is for champions, so we need you to come out swinging from the beginning because champions are built on the lessons you learn today. You've got to swing those bats!"

Mrs. Kerrington joined the circle. "We play at nine o'clock in the morning, field three."

"Girls, be here at eight, ready to play," Coach Kory said.

"Bring it in," Coach Dave said. It was the Lady Tigers' ritual to start and end every day by giving a cheer to softball. The girls stood and pushed their right hands into the center of the circle on top one another.

"One, two, three," they called in unison, raising their hands into the air on the cry of, "Softball!"

The parents gathered around the girls as the group broke up.

Wrapping his arms around his daughter, Master Sergeant Edward Clark gave her a tight squeeze. "Good game, Pumpkin!"

Margie took in her father's scent as she hugged him tightly. He smelled like jet fuel and oil. Margie had grown up around airplanes all her life and loved that smell. It was comforting to her. She slowly looked up to find her dad's face.

"I screwed up," she grumbled.

He smiled down at her. "Did you learn something from it?" he asked.

He always asked questions like that.

"Yes, sir," she replied.

"Then chalk it up to a lesson learned and plan for improvement."

Margie's mom gave her a quick squeeze. "You did fine, honey. You had some really nice plays. Keep that in mind, too."

Margie felt small hands grab at her legs. She turned and laughed as her baby sister clung to her pants, trying to pull herself up.

Margie bent over and picked Tara up, bouncing her in her arms. "Were you watching, Squirt?" Margie asked her sister in a playful voice. "Did you learn from my mistake, too?"

Tara giggled and patted Margie's head.

Chapter 2

The next night, Margie heard hushed whispers coming from the living room. Her father had put Tara to bed an hour ago and Margie was in her room reading. The tournament had ended well, but she was tired.

Her parents were downstairs watching television. At least that was what Margie had thought until the sound of her mother shushing her father had cut through her concentration.

Ears perked, Margie quietly climbed off her bed and walked closer to the door.

"How long?" she heard her mother ask in quiet frustration.

"Six or seven months," her father answered, just as quietly.

There were no sounds for a very long time.

"When are you going to tell Margie?"

There was another long pause before she heard her dad's voice again. "I don't leave for another few days. I think we should wait. I don't want her to be upset more than necessary."

"More than necessary?" her mother's voice rose. Then she dropped her voice again, "What do you consider necessary? She's going to be heartbroken. She struggled a lot last time you were gone."

"She's older now. It should be easier on her."

Her mother's voice cracked with emotion. "A young lady needs her father. She's eleven! She is going to be starting middle school, and all the drama that entails."

"It's my turn to go. We've been fortunate that I haven't deployed in the last few years. My last assignment as an instructor just put off the inevitable."

She heard movement from the living room. Then a door opened and closed. A few minutes later, she heard the door open and close again. There were no further sounds from downstairs.

Margie slipped over to her bedroom window which looked out over the backyard. Peeling back the curtain slightly, she saw her father hugging her mother on the back porch.

She let the curtain fall back in place and retraced her steps to the bed. Crawling under the covers, she buried her head in her pillow and tried not to think about her father leaving for such a long time. Her emotions raced between disappointment and anger. How could he do this to them?

Monday afternoon, Margie sat in the living room flipping through TV channels. Her cell buzzed. Margie ignored it.

It buzzed again.

Her mother looked up from her book with a questioning look.

Reluctantly, Margie dropped the remote, picking up the cell her parents had given her for her birthday two years previously. It was right after they had moved into this house, and her father had started traveling so much with work. Her dad said with the phone they could stay in touch no matter where he was. It didn't really work. His work schedule made it hard to talk. They did text, though. Her dad didn't really get the whole texting language, but he tried.

Margie glanced at the screen. "Trish wants to meet for yogurt," she told her mother without interest. "Sally and Nikki are going too."

"Sounds like fun. What time does she want to meet? It has to be after dinner. Dad will be home soon."

"I don't feel like going."

"Since when do you not feel like frozen yogurt?" her mother said with a laugh.

When Margie didn't join her, she asked, "What's bothering you, honey?"

Margie felt herself getting angry. She tried to stay calm, but when she thought of her dad leaving again—and not wanting to tell her—she only got madder.

He had been traveling more lately, but they were short trips, only weeks at a time. She couldn't imagine not seeing her dad for six whole months!

"Dad's leaving, isn't he?" Margie blurted out.

The look on her mother's face was confirmation enough. Her eyes filled with tears as she reached a hand out to stroke Margie's hair. "Baby, he's not going for very long."

"That's what you always say!" Margie yelled, jumping from her seat. "Then he misses Christmas or my birthday. He's going to miss Tara learning to talk!"

Running to her room, she slammed the door and threw herself facedown onto the bed. As she lay there stewing in her anger, she became aware of the uncomfortable lump pressing into her ribcage. She rolled over and tugged at the object.

Lammy. Her dad had given her this now well-worn stuffed lamb when she was about Tara's age. Her mother had restuffed the white, fuzzy cloth several times already, but Lammy looked like she could use another refill.

There was a light knock at her door. "Can I come in?" she heard her dad ask.

Margie jammed the stuffed animal under her blanket and sat up. "Sure," she said glumly.

Her dad pushed the door open. "You know, I hear these can't slam if they are taken off the hinges."

Margie cringed. She had gotten in trouble for slamming doors before. One day she came home from school and her bedroom door was gone. Her father never said anything to her about it, and he didn't have to. It was two weeks before she had her door, and her privacy, back.

"I'm sorry," she offered.

"You're forgiven. But I think it's your mom you owe the apology to."

"Yes, sir," she said sheepishly.

Sitting on the edge of her bed, he covered her hand with his own. "You know why I have to go away, don't you?"

She shrugged.

"There are people out in this world hurting other people. I don't like to see that happening."

"But they're way far away!" she blurted out. "Why do you care?"

He sighed. "Those people need our help. If you or your mom or your sister needed help, wouldn't you want people to come?"

"They wouldn't need to if you were here."

He considered before he answered. "Some of those folks don't have anyone like me. They don't have anyone to stand up for them. Or they haven't learned to do it for themselves. We go to teach them."

Margie refused to look at her father. They had talks like this before. He had warned her that someday he would have to go overseas. She knew the logic behind it, but that didn't make it any easier.

He gave her arm a playful shake. "You're not that different from me, you

know? Someday, you'll surprise yourself."
He stood up, "For now, you need to go talk
to your mom. This isn't easy on her either."
He walked out, leaving the bedroom door
open.

Margie flopped backwards on the bed
and stared at the ceiling. She willed herself
not to cry. Why should she be upset? She
was too old for this! She didn't need him, she
thought. But a lump found its way into her
throat as a tear trickled down her cheek.

Shifting her body, she reached under her
and pulled out the white, stuffed lamb again.
She held it in front of her face with both
hands. "You won't leave, will you,
Lammy?"

Chapter 3

Margie's dad dropped her off at practice Thursday night. Trish waved her over to where she was playing catch with Sally and Nikki.

"Why so glum?" Nikki asked Margie when she joined them.

Margie shrugged. She caught the ball Nikki threw her and tossed it back.

"We missed you for yogurt. Didn't you get my text?" Trish asked.

"Yeah, I got it. I just wasn't in the mood."

"Are you sick or something? You love frozen yogurt!" Sally teased her.

Margie gave a weak smile.

Nikki stopped throwing and walked toward Margie. "What's really up? You aren't yourself."

Sally and Trish stopped their game of catch and joined the other girls.

Kicking at the grass, Margie looked down at her feet. "My dad's leaving again," she said.

"Leaving? For where?" Trish asked.

"Afghanistan."

"But he's in the Air Force," Nikki said.

Margie looked up at her. "It's more than just the Army in Afghanistan, you know."

"No, I didn't know," Nikki admitted.

"Dad takes care of the planes that are over there. He's a great mechanic," Margie said with a note of pride in her voice.

"Is it dangerous?" Sally asked curiously.

"It can be. There are people that don't want them there, and they aren't shy about it."

The girls fell into silence.

"Ladies, you are supposed to be warming up your arms, not your mouths," Coach Dave yelled from the bench.

The girls scattered back to their positions, each lost in her own thoughts.

Saturday's tournament started off well for the Lady Tigers. They won their first game 6-2 and their second game 10-1.

As they prepared to take the field for their third game, Coach Kory called them together. "You've done well so far, but don't get overconfident," he cautioned. "You're good ball players, but you're a great team! Work together and we can pull this off. But what's the most important thing to remember?"

"To have fun!" the girls shouted together.

"Okay, call it off," Coach Sam said, putting his hand into the center of the circle.

Each girl put her hand into the circle. Coach Sam counted, "One, two, three…"

"Softball!" the girls yelled, throwing their hands up in the air.

They jogged out to their respective places on the field. Margie took second base. Trish was in her usual spot in centerfield. Sally was getting a break from pitching and stood beside Margie at first base. Nikki was still behind the plate.

Margie was glad to be surrounded by her friends. It was great to be on the field playing softball on such a beautiful day. It kept her distracted. She knew it wouldn't be long before her dad had to leave.

For now, he was there in the stands with Margie's mother and little sister. She saw him chatting with Trish's dad while they waited for the game to start.

The first four innings were very quick, with only one girl from each team actually getting on base. All the others batters either struck out or were easily thrown out after hitting the ball to the infield. Now at the top of the fourth inning, the Lady Tigers were once again in the field.

The first batter hit a line drive up the middle, shooting over the second base bag into centerfield. Trish scooped it up and threw it to Margie at second base.

The second batter swung at the first pitch and missed. On the next pitch, the batter squared for the bunt. This time, Margie didn't hesitate. As the pitcher and first baseman rushed for the ball, Margie ran to cover first base. The throw from Sally was right on target, but Margie didn't wait to hear the umpire's call. She drew the ball from her glove and winged it to third base, where the runner was inbound. As Nicole Carter took the throw at third base, she swept her arm back in a beautiful arc, catching the runner's sliding feet a foot in front of the bag.

"Out!" the umpire yelled.

The crowd cheered as the Tigers rushed to the pitcher's mound where they exchanged high fives.

Cupping his hands to his mouth to project his voice above the ruckus, Margie's dad shouted, "Way to go, Pumpkin!"

Grinning from ear-to-ear, Margie took her place back at second base.

A strikeout finished the inning, and the Tigers prepared to hit.

Riding on the wave of adrenaline, the girls focused their energy on the bat.

"Girls, show me the champions you are!" Coach Sam encouraged them.

The first two girls hit singles into the outfield that put them on first and second base. The third batter struck out. Margie was the fourth batter for the inning, with one out.

She tried not to look at him, but she couldn't stop herself from stealing a glance at her father as she walked to the plate. He was clapping and cheering her on.

The first pitch was a ball. On the second pitch, the coach gave her the bunt take sign. That meant she was to fake a bunt to draw the third and first basemen in, but stop at the last minute from hitting the ball. If done well, the runners would be able to steal, putting them in scoring position.

The ruse worked as planned, and the runner on second was able to steal third base, while the runner on first advanced to second.

Margie risked another glance at her dad. He was on the phone now, talking urgently while trying to keep his eye on the game. She saw him shake his head and turn away.

Stepping into the batter's box, Margie tried to concentrate. If this was the last game her dad was going to see, she wanted to make him proud. With the next pitch, she extended her arms and swung with all her might. She caught the ball dead center, sending it sailing over the right fielder's head. As she rounded first and pushed to second, she saw Coach Kory next to third base waving her on.

Stretching her legs and giving it everything she had, she sped toward third. Margie could tell from the reaction on the third baseman's face that the ball was inbound. She knew she would have to slide. She hit the ground smoothly, laying down on her right side. She felt her foot hit the bag, then the ball smash into the center of her back, knocking the wind out of her.

The umpire called her safe, immediately followed by a timeout. Coach Kory rushed to her side and knelt beside her.

"You okay?" he asked, looking worried, but excited.

Margie nodded, but didn't move otherwise.

The coach patiently waited for her to catch her breath. "Not too shabby," he said, making small talk as he grinned at her. "If a triple is all you can do…"

She smiled back and started to push herself up. He grabbed her hand and hauled her to her feet.

Both sides clapped to see she wasn't injured. While she brushed off her uniform, she tried to look nonchalantly at the crowd for her father. Coach Kory caught on, and pointed discretely to her dad, standing at the top of the bleachers, cheering louder than anyone.

The timer went off, sounding that time had expired and the game ended. The Tigers won, two to nothing.

They would be in the championship game the next morning.

Chapter 4

Sunday is for champions, but Margie didn't feel like being a champion today. She watched as her dad loaded his duffle bag into the car. He slammed the trunk lid closed and walked toward the house. With his uniform sleeves rolled up just above his elbows, Margie could see the muscles in his forearms. She noticed the scar on his right arm where a wrench had once slipped, allowing a piece of the equipment he was working on to fall and slice his arm. He had told her the white mark was a reminder so that he would never make the same mistake again.

Already dressed in her Tigers uniform, Margie sat on the front steps and watched her dad as he prepared to leave. He hugged Tara and kissed her face until she giggled. Her mom stood with her arm around his waist, head resting on his shoulder.

"Come here, Gloomy," he called to Margie. "You aren't going to let me leave with that sad face being what I remember on my flight."

Pulling herself to her feet, she felt as though she were walking through molasses to cross the few steps to where her family waited. Her mom took Tara in her arms and Margie fell into her father. Hugging him around the waist, she squeezed as if she could keep him there by sheer will power.

"Don't break me," he teased, though he held onto her with equal force. "Keep your phone charged, okay?"

She nodded, not trusting herself to speak.

"And good luck at your game today. Send me a picture of you with the winning trophy."

"I don't feel like playing today," Margie said.

Squeezing her a last time, Margie's father released her, kneeling down to get on eye-level with his daughter. "You might not feel like it," he said, "but those girls are counting on you. Today isn't about you. It's about the team. Remember Spock's famous quote, 'The needs of the many—'"

"'—outweigh the needs of the few,'" she finished, smiling slightly at the reference to one of their favorite movies.

"Will you send me the photo?"

"Yes, sir," she replied.

"I love you," he said.

"Not as much as I love you."

He stood up again and gave Tara a kiss on the forehead. He kissed his wife warmly and whispered something to her.

She smiled. "Me too," she said. "Call us often."

One last quick hug for Margie and Master Sergeant Clark got into his car and drove away.

Margie felt the tears slide down her cheeks as she looked up to see that her mother's eyes were moist too. But when her mom spoke, Margie heard a forced cheerfulness that Margie was sure was to keep Tara from sensing her distress. "Okay, girls, I think we have a game to get to!"

Margie dumped her bat bag with her gear into the dugout and watched her team prepare to defend against the next batter. The scoreboard showed that the game was in the second inning with no runs for either team.

"You didn't miss a thing," Coach Sam said as Margie took a seat next to him against the fence.

She had arrived late so that she could say goodbye to her dad, but she was grateful Coach Sam didn't mention it.

Sally was on the mound preparing for the next pitch.

"Watch the batter. See where she's standing?" Coach Sam said without taking his eyes off the field.

Margie looked. "She's standing in the front of the batter's box, closer to the pitcher than normal," she answered.

"What do you think that means?"

"Bunt!" she said as the batter turned her body in the box and dropped her bat so it was parallel with the ground at waist level.

The batter caught the high pitch under the ball and it popped up in the air. Nikki, who was catching behind the plate, stood and caught it easily for the third out.

Coach Sam clapped Margie on the back as he rose to greet the girls when they came off the field.

As the girls bustled about getting ready for their turn to bat, Sally approached Margie. "How'd it go?"

Margie shrugged. She didn't trust herself to talk about it. Obviously, her best friends knew that her dad had left today. She suspected the coaches had told the whole team, since no one else asked her why she was late.

Nikki approached, stripping off the chest protector she wore behind the plate. She was covered in dust that turned to mud when she splashed cold water on her face.

"Tough game already?" Margie teased her.

"Hot already," Nikki replied. She turned back to the field and cheered for Trish as she approached the plate. "Get us started, Trish!"

Trish settled into the batter's box, waiting for the pitch she wanted to hit. She sent the third pitch sailing into left center field, running to second base before the ball was thrown back into the infield.

Margie was on her feet cheering, momentarily forgetting that she wouldn't see her dad until sometime after Christmas.

Dad, u were right. Took #1. Like the pic? Miss u already.

After hitting send on the text, Margie stuck her cell phone in her back pocket. She grabbed her bat bag and walked with her friends to the parking lot.

"I think this calls for a celebration!" Sally declared.

"I agree!" Trish joined in. "Extra sprinkles with our yogurt!"

Margie laughed along with them, but she didn't feel much like celebrating.

With a one-armed hug, Nikki drug Margie toward the waiting parents. "Mrs. Clark, can Margie go with us for frozen yogurt? Dad will bring her home."

Mrs. Clark smiled at her daughter. "I think that would be a wonderful idea." She reached into her pocket and handed Margie some cash. "I expect change!" she said with a wink.

Margie dumped her bag in her mom's car before following Sally and Nikki.

The girls climbed into the backseat. "Sorry I'm being a downer," Margie said.

"It's understandable," Sally said. "My dad really gets on my nerves sometimes, but it would be tough to go months without seeing him."

"I'm sitting right here!" Mr. Andrews said playfully from the driver's seat. "And I believe it's not a good idea to insult your date before he pays."

The girls laughed and buckled in.

Fellow teammates were already in line when they arrived. They joined the group, and soon were eating and replaying all the top action moments from the weekend.

"Ladies," Coach Kory greeted them. "Did you save any for us old guys?"

"Guess you need to be quicker," Trish teased.

Playfully he tapped her on top of her head. They all giggled.

Conversation died down as they all scraped the bottoms of their now empty cups. Tammy and Amy were sitting at the next table. Amy leaned over and said quietly to Margie, "Sorry to hear about your dad deploying."

A lump formed in Margie's throat. She chased it down with her last spoonful of yogurt. "He'll be back soon," she said. "Quicker if the bad guys cooperate."

They smiled with her.

Somewhere a phone dinged. All the girls reached for their pockets. Margie pulled hers out triumphantly. "It's from Dad!" she said with excitement.

Just landed. Congrats! Great pic! Keep them coming. Luv u.

"He got the picture I sent," Margie told the others.

"What picture?" Trish asked.

Margie pulled it up and handed Trish the phone.

"This is good. Will you send it to me?"

Taking the phone back, Margie typed in Trish's number and hit send.

Seconds later, Trish's phone chirped. She typed in a number and forwarded the photo on.

"Who'd you send it to?" Nikki asked.

"My dad. Probably a good idea to keep him interested."

"Sorry he didn't make the games today, Trish," Sally said.

Trish shrugged. "He came yesterday. That's pretty good for him." She didn't seem at all disappointed.

Chapter 5

Margie's dad had been gone almost six weeks. There was a lot of extra work to do around the house, helping her mother with chores and taking care of Tara. Margie didn't really mind, though. She knew her mom needed a break once in a while and besides, she discovered that her mom let her do a lot more grown-up things than she did before her dad left. She got to go into the grocery store by herself—with her mom waiting in the car, of course. And she got Skype on her phone so she could see her dad, and not just text him. She was kind of liking the changes.

The doorbell rang. Margie rushed to answer it.

Swinging the door open, she was excited to see her three best friends on the front porch. She grabbed a sleeping bag from Sally's hand and ushered them all inside.

"Mom! Mrs. Andrews is here!" Margie called up the steps. She waited until her mom joined Mrs. Andrews, then the four girls raced off to the basement.

"This is great!" Trish said, looking around at the spacious room. An overstuffed couch with large pillows stood against the back wall, with a large screen TV on the opposite wall. Multi-colored, huge bags covered in cloth were placed randomly about the room.

"Drop your stuff anywhere. We're going to sleep down here," Margie said.

"What's this?" Trish asked, dropping into one of the giant cushions.

"Foof chairs. Great, aren't they?" Margie answered. "They're like beanbag chairs, but with foam or something instead of beans."

Sally and Nikki each plopped down on their own.

Nikki snuggled into hers and gave an exaggerated sigh. "Wake me in a few days," she said with her eyes closed.

Margie grabbed a pillow from the couch and threw it at her.

"Hey," she yelled playfully.

That started an all-out pillow fight that ended when Mrs. Clark called down the stairs. "Girls, come on up. We're getting ready to leave."

Mrs. Andrews and Margie's mom were going to the movies. The girls had agreed to stay home with Tara to give Margie's mom some grownup time.

The girls climbed the steps, following Margie into the kitchen. On wobbly legs, Tara did her version of a run and clamped on to Trish's leg. Trish laughed and reached down to pick her up.

"You're getting bigger every time I see you," Trish said to Tara, "and heavier!"

They all laughed.

When the girls were standing dutifully in front of the adults, Mrs. Clark went over the ground rules.

"You are here to take care of Tara. That means, what you want to do comes second. She needs to be fed, then brush her teeth, and get her ready for bed."

"Story!" Tara exclaimed.

"Yes, and a story," Mrs. Clark agreed.

"I'll do that," said Sally. "I love to read."

"I already gave her a bath so don't worry about that. After she's asleep—and I mean after," she emphasized, "you can watch TV or play cards in the living room. Don't go back downstairs until we get home. You might not be able to hear Tara from the basement."

The girls all nodded their understanding.

"Tara," Mrs. Clark said to the toddler, "you listen to the big girls. No fussing about bedtime."

She buried her face in Trish's shoulder.

Mrs. Clark gave her a quick peck on her chubby cheek. To the others, she said, "Call us if you have any problems or questions."

Mrs. Andrews smiled. "We won't be out too late. Then you girls can have your slumber party."

As the door closed behind the ladies, Margie reached over and tickled Tara's belly. "What do you want to do first, Squirt?" she asked.

Tara instantly wiggled out of Trish's arms. "Hide and seek!" she cried. "Go!" With that, her little legs propelled her from the room.

The other girls laughed. "Okay, I'll be it," Nikki volunteered. Sitting down in a kitchen chair, she closed her eyes and began counting. "One, two, three, four,…"

Sally, Margie, and Trish scattered. As they moved through the living room, they heard a giggle coming from behind the couch. They moved past and up the steps.

"Ready or not, here I come!" they heard Nikki call through the house.

"Here I am!" they heard Tara's high-pitched voice call out, jumping out of her hiding place.

"Come on. You're on my team now," Nikki said, taking her hand. "Let's find your sister."

Chapter 6

The girls played multiple rounds of hide and seek, then they colored fire trucks, dolls, and birds while Margie made macaroni and cheese for dinner.

After dinner, Tara dutifully brushed her teeth under the close supervision of Margie. Tara insisted that Margie sing the happy birthday song so Tara would know how long to brush. Hiding around the corner, Sally recorded it on her cell phone to play back later in the evening.

When it was finally time to put Tara to bed, all four girls followed her to her room to pick out a story. Tara picked out *Thomas the Train*. Scrambling under the covers, she motioned for Sally to sit beside her. The others sat on the floor against the walls.

As Thomas saved the day, the toddler wasn't the only one yawning. By the time Sally reached the end, Tara was out and the others didn't look too far behind. Quietly getting up, they tiptoed down the stairs to the living room.

"That was a lot of fun," Nikki said.

"It's a lot more fun with you guys here," Margie added. "I don't mind helping with Tara, but it does get boring."

"Do you have any popcorn?" Trish asked. "I'm still hungry."

The girls headed back to the kitchen. They searched through the cupboard and came up with interesting combinations of food to dare each other to eat. Taking their bounty, they sat down at the kitchen table to play cards.

Before they knew it, they heard the front door open. "Girls, we're back!" Mrs. Clark called.

"In here," they answered in unison, then broke into fits of laughter.

Taking in the variety of food and empty soda cans on the table, Mrs. Andrews laughed herself. "Good luck tonight! They aren't ever going to get to sleep!" She kissed her daughters. "Be good. I'll see you in the morning."

"Good night," the kids spoke together again, which started another round of laughter.

"Clean up and then you can go downstairs," Mrs. Clark said.

With a flurry of activity, the girls put their dirty dishes in the sink and wiped off the table. Minutes later they had each claimed a Foof chair.

"What time is it?" Sally asked.

Glancing at her watch, Trish answered, "Almost eleven o'clock."

Margie sat up straight. "Let's call my dad!" she exclaimed excitedly. "He should just be getting up. I'm not usually awake this late to be able to call him."

"What time is it in Afghanistan?" Nikki asked.

"Almost seven in the morning. It's perfect! He'll be getting ready for work."

Margie dug her cell phone out of her back pocket and started the Skype app. As the phone rang, the others gathered around behind her so they could all see the screen.

Master Sargent Clark's worried face filled the display. "What's wrong?"

"Hi, Mr. Clark!" the girls called out, then started to giggle again.

Relieved, Margie's father smiled broadly. "Good morning, girls! Or should I say good night? Isn't it a little late there?"

"We're having a sleepover," Margie explained.

"I figured as much," he replied.

"Mrs. Clark went out with our mom to the movies," Sally chimed in.

"We got to watch Tara!" Nikki added.

"She's in bed though," Trish assured him.

"I'm so glad you girls are there for Margie's mom. She's a special woman and I need someone to watch out for her. I'll bet the other people in my unit wish they had four young ladies like yourselves on their home team."

The girls laughed at his softball reference. Then they took turns telling him about the best plays at the last tournament.

Finally he had to cut them off. "Girls, you have made my day. I wish I didn't have to, but I must go to work now."

The girls grumbled, but grudgingly said their good nights. Trish, Sally, and Nikki went to brush their teeth to give Margie some time alone with her dad.

When they came back in the room, Margie was grinning ear-to-ear.

"What's going on?" Nikki asked.

"I have an idea!" Margie proclaimed.

Chapter 7

The snap of the balls hitting the leather mitts filled the air as the girls warmed up at practice a few days later.

"That's a lot of kids in one place," Trish commented.

"If we get enough girls to help—" Margie's words were cut off as she jumped to catch a wild throw. "—it will be easy enough to manage," she finished when she had regained her balance.

The girls were still brainstorming and building on Margie's idea of finding a way to do something special for the families when one of the parents was deployed. Margie's talk with her father during the sleepover had sparked an idea that she couldn't shake. Determined that she had to do something, she had enlisted the help of her best friends.

"How will we keep them entertained?" Sally asked.

"Movies?" Nikki offered.

"Crafts?" Trish put in.

They fell silent into their own thoughts as they continued to throw the softball back and forth.

"Line up at home plate!" Coach Dave yelled.

Putting their discussion on hold, the girls jogged to home plate to start their practice drills.

"No way you can hit the bucket on the first try!" Trish taunted Margie playfully from across the field. The Lady Tigers were finishing their practice with their bucket challenge. The coach laid a bucket on its side at home plate while the girls lined up at the second base bag.

Coach Kory handed Margie a softball. "You have three chances to hit the bucket, and I'll give you a point for each hit."

"What if it goes in the bucket?" Nikki asked.

The coach laughed. "If it goes in, I'll give you three points!"

Margie dropped the ball into her glove and wiped the hair out of her eyes with her throwing hand.

"C'mon, Margie! You can do it!"

As the girls urged her on, Margie threw the ball with all her might. With once bounce, it smacked on the rim of the white plastic, spinning it around the plate. The team let out a cheer.

"Lucky shot!" Trish teased, retrieving the ball from the backstop where it had rolled to a stop. She reset the bucket and threw the ball back to Margie.

"You know I can do whatever I set my mind to," she told her friend with a grin. Two more throws—two more hits. Then it was Sally's turn.

Each girl got her shot at the bucket, but in the end Nikki was declared the winner. With a catcher's arm, it was hard to beat her accuracy.

As the girls cleaned up the dugout, Sally commented, "That was a lot of fun."

"It sure doesn't feel like practice when the coaches come up with cool drills for us," Nikki said.

"That's it!" Margie exclaimed.

"That's what?" Trish asked.

"Why don't we teach them how to play softball?"

"Teach who?" Tammy asked. She was stuffing her gear into her bag.

"Margie wants to do something special for some of the kids on base whose mom or dad is deployed," Trish explained to the Tigers' first baseman.

"That's a neat idea," Tammy said.

Margie was practically jumping up and down in her excitement. "We can have the parents drop them off for a few hours on a weekend. We can teach them the basics, and do some drills with them."

"How many kids and how old are they?" Nikki asked. "Their skill levels are going to be all over the map."

Margie thought about it.

"We can divide them into age groups," Sally suggested. "But we'd probably need a lot more help."

"I'll help," Tammy said.

"Count me in," Amy said. She had been listening as they gathered their things.

"I'll bet a bunch of the girls would," Trish said. "Maybe it can be a team thing. We need to ask Coach Kory."

The girls raced off to catch the coach as he was loading things into his truck.

Chapter 8

Margie sat at the kitchen table, hard at work. Coach Kory had agreed to help with softball clinic. Margie's mom had received permission to give her the social roster from her dad's squadron that listed all the names of the members of the unit and their email addresses.

Trish sat across from Margie, decorating a poster the girls had designed to advertise the clinic. "What did your dad say when you told him about your idea?"

"He loved it," Margie said without looking up. Working on her mother's laptop, she was crafting an email for her mom to send to the squadron families to invite them to the event in two weeks' time.

"How does this sound?" Margie asked. "Need a break? Let the Lady Tigers spend some time with your kids, teaching them the basics of softball and baseball. It's heathy for your child and for you!"

"You need to add something that says it's free," Trish said.

The doorbell rang. A few minutes later Sally and Nikki entered the kitchen. Nikki carried a large, dusty box. "Hey! Look what we found in the garage," Nikki said. "It's a bunch of old stuff dad used when he coached us in tee ball. He said we could have it."

"Awesome!" Margie said. She typed a few more lines into the email while Sally started pulling things out of the box, spreading them on the kitchen floor.

Finished with her typing, Margie gave the sisters her full attention.

Sally held up a baseball glove that barely covered her hand. "Look how cute!"

Trish got down on her knees beside the box, rummaging through the treasures. "I count at least twelve tee balls," she announced.

"And four gloves, two batting helmets, and some whiffle balls."

"There's a batting tee in the garage still," Sally added. "Probably some bats too. We'll check when we get home."

"This is great. Tell your dad I said thanks," Margie said.

"Do we have any idea how many kids yet?" Nikki asked.

"Mom figures there are about 120 families in the squadron. Only about 40 of those have smaller children that aren't babies. She said some of those families probably won't be in town. Sometimes when one parent deploys, the family uses that time to go visit grandparents. That way the mom or dad doesn't have to do everything by themselves."

"Are you going away?" Trish sounded a little concerned.

"Nah. We're used to this. Dad has deployed before."

"So what do you want us to do?" Sally asked, tossing the items back into the box and wiping her hands on her shorts.

"Well," Margie said, "I just finished the email. Trish is making a poster to hang in the squadron building. Can you make a list of what we still need? Nikki, can you help me outline the drills you think we can do with the kids? We'll need some kind of schedule."

The girls grabbed paper and pencils from the stack on the table and got down to work.

Chapter 9

The sky was clear and sunny with a slight breeze—perfect weather for playing ball. The Lady Tigers gathered on the pitcher's mound, but this time, instead of Coach Kory giving the pep talk, the team clustered around Margie.

"Tammy, you and Amy will work on hitting off the tee. Make sure they keep their helmets on, even if they aren't swinging the bat. Trish and Angie, you guys run the soft toss. Sal and Nikki, throw some short fly balls. One of you can throw while the other shows them the right way to catch." Margie went through the rest of the assignments.

"How many kids are coming?" one of the Tigers asked.

"Thirty kids between the ages of six and ten," Margie answered. "That's why we are playing on two fields."

The coaches stood next to the bleachers and talked with the parents. They had big grins on their faces and seemed more laid back than usual.

"Margie," Coach Dave called, "I think they're here."

The Tigers ran to their stations outside the fence to welcome the kids. Margie stood at the check-in table, welcoming each parent and child. While her teammates took the children onto the field, Margie had the parents sign a piece of paper explaining the safety rules.

After waiting a few more minutes with no new arrivals, Margie jogged onto the field and called everyone's attention. "Thanks for spending your Saturday with us," she began. "We're excited you're here. We hope we can teach you some of what our coaches have taught us. Let's start with introductions." She began by introducing the three Lady Tiger coaches and then each of her teammates, pointing out their specialty on the field.

Then she broke the kids into smaller groups, made sure everyone had equipment, and sent them into the outfield to warm up.

As the kids followed the older girls to their places, Margie went back to the dugout to put down her clipboard. Her mom met her at the bench.

Mrs. Clark captured her in a hug. Margie hugged her back, taken by surprise at the spontaneous show of affection. When she pulled back, Margie saw the tears in her mother's eyes.

"Mom, are you okay?"

With a weak smile, her mom replied, "I'm fine."

"Is dad okay?" Margie's voice rose in panic.

"Oh, Honey, he's fine," her mother quickly reassured her. With a larger smile, but her eyes still wet, she added, "He will be so proud of you."

Margie felt the heat in her cheeks, and the warmth of knowing her mom was right.

"Excuse me?"

Margie and her mother turned to the voice coming from outside the dugout.

"Are you here for the clinic?" Margie asked in her most professional voice.

"Oh, good. We're in the right place. I was worried we'd missed it," the older lady said. She rested a grandmotherly hand on the shoulder of a young boy about eight years old and gave him a gentle nudge forward.

"I'm Anita Grafton. This is my grandson Jake." When the boy didn't respond, Jake's grandmother and Mrs. Clark exchanged a knowing glance.

Mrs. Grafton prompted him. "Can you say hello?"

He stared resolutely at the ground.

Margie stepped forward and bent down to be eye-level with the little boy. He had a small frame and dark brown hair, and wore shorts with his red Minecraft T-shirt. A baseball cap was pulled low over his eyes.

Lifting the bill of his cap just enough to get his attention, Margie asked, "Do you like baseball?"

"This isn't baseball. You're a girl and girls don't play baseball." He crossed his arms defiantly across his chest. "This is stupid."

Rather than taking offense, Margie pretended to consider his reply carefully. "I'm pretty sure I know how to throw a baseball. It's a lot like throwing a softball, only throwing a baseball is easier."

Jake's eyes snapped up, "No way. Baseball's a lot harder."

Margie stood up. "A lot of things that are similar between baseball and softball, but today we are going to play T-ball."

"T-ball's for babies," Jake said.

"You already know everything there is to know about T-ball? Good. We could use a pro like you." Margie turned her back and walked toward the field.

When he didn't follow right away, she stopped and turned, "Are you coming? Or are you afraid I can throw a baseball farther than you can?"

Without a glance back at his grandmother, Jake jogged to catch up with Margie, then fell into step behind her, not wanting to portray agreement. Margie pretended to ignore him, but the small grin on her face showed that she was pleased with this bit of progress. His fierce determination might just prove to be a real asset to the team, she thought.

When the last of the children had left the ball field, the Lady Tigers sprawled in the outfield grass.

"That was exhausting," Tammy said as she rolled onto her back.

The breeze cooled the girls as they passed around water bottles, splashing some on their heads and necks.

"But a lot of fun," Amy chimed in. "Great idea, Margie."

"Absolutely," others agreed, throwing in their comments.

"That Jake is one tough cookie," Trish said.

Sal asked, "Was that the boy in the Minecraft T-shirt?"

"Yep. His mom is one of the pilots in my dad's squadron," Margie explained. "This is the first time she's been away for so long. And he's only eight."

"He didn't want to try anything."

"Yeah, he just stood on the side and watched," Nikki said.

"It's a shame he didn't join in. The others seemed to have fun," Amy said.

"Hey look!" Tammy said, pointing at the group of adults walking across the infield. Two parents carried a cooler between them. Others carried trays of food.

The girls sat up to see what was going on.

"Ladies, we thought you might need some nourishment after all that work," Mrs. Andrews said.

"You did a great job out there," Coach Kory said. "I'm very proud of you."

Trays of home baked cookies were passed around, each girl grabbing two or three. Gatorades or juice bottles were tossed to each Tiger.

"I do have some good news for you," Margie's mom said. "You did such a super job out there that the kids want to know when you're going to do it again."

A groan went up from the girls, but there was a smile underneath, and Margie could tell that this wouldn't be their only clinic.

Chapter 10

As Margie sat at the kitchen table going over the sign-up list for the Lady Tigers' second clinic, she noticed a name missing. "What's up with that Jake kid?"

Margie's mom looked up from the book she was reading. "I don't know. Why?"

"He didn't sign up to come to the clinic."

"If I remember correctly, he didn't seem that interested in the first one," her mom said gently.

"I think he was interested. He just pretended not to be." Margie thought for a minute, then she dug through the notes from the first clinic. "Mom, he only lives a few blocks away. Think I can go over and talk to him?"

Mrs. Clark smiled lovingly at her daughter. "I think that's a nice idea. Don't pressure him though. If he doesn't want to come, don't make him."

"I think I'll go now. I can ride my bike and be back before dinner."

"Do you want me to drive you over?"

"No. It's not far. Besides, I think he'll do better without a mom around."

"Take your cell phone with you and text me when you get there," her mother said.

Margie jumped up and kissed her mother's cheek.

A few minutes later, she was peddling around the block, looking at the house numbers. When she saw the red brick house set back on a wide lawn, she turned into the long, circular driveway. Leaning her bike against a lamp post, she texted her mom as she walked up the four steps and rang the doorbell.

The elderly lady Margie remembered seeing at the ball field opened the door. Confused at first, then a flicker of recognition registered in her eyes. "You're the little girl from the clinic, aren't you?"

Margie nodded, although she didn't much appreciate being called "little."

"I noticed Jake didn't sign up for the clinic we're having in a few weeks."

Jake's grandma glanced back into the house. Then, turning back to Margie she said quietly, "Jake's struggling with his mother being gone. He's an only child, and he and his mother are very close."

"The first time my dad left was before my sister was born. I remember thinking he was mad at me."

"Now Jake acts like he's mad at everyone, but don't take it personally. He really isn't. He's just hurt."

"Jake?" His grandmother called into the house. "There's someone here to see you."

The young boy took his time getting to the door, but Margie waited patiently, practicing what she was going to say.

When he finally saw Margie, he stopped in his tracks.

"Why don't you two go out to the swings?" his grandma suggested. "I'll bring out some lemonade."

Jake walked past Margie without acknowledging her. Margie followed him around the house to the wooden structure in the backyard that held two traditional swings with fake boards as seats, as well as a tire, suspended by three chains. A colorful, hard plastic slide twisted its way from the flat deck on top of the fort to a sandpit at the bottom.

"This is awesome," Margie said, and she meant it. She plopped down on one of the plastic seats. She slowly began pumping her legs, waiting to see what Jake would do.

He climbed onto the tire swing without saying a word.

"What did you think of the clinic?" Margie asked.

"It was lame," were Jake's first words to her since her arrival.

"Sorry you thought so," Margie said. "I had a lot of fun. So did the girls on my team."

"It wasn't real baseball," Jake said.

"It wasn't meant to be," she explained. "It was a clinic. The idea is to help with skills that are used in baseball or softball. And just to have fun."

The tiny shoulders inside his tee shirt went up and down.

"How does that swing work?" Margie asked, trying to draw him out.

"It's just a swing," he said with disinterest.

"But how do you make it go? You can't pump your legs like you do on this one."

Jake rolled his eyes and climbed off. "Get on," he directed.

"Me?"

"Who else?" he said with exaggerated impatience.

Margie made a good show of not knowing the proper way to sit in the tire so that Jake had to teach her. She got her legs caught and pretended to fall out.

A giggle escaped from Jake before he caught himself. Still, he smiled as Margie righted herself and put her feet on the tire opposite where she sat.

"Hold on," he warned. With that, Jake grabbed two of the chains and began running in a tight circle, dragging the tire with him.

Margie watched as the three chains twisted on themselves, starting from where it connected to the wooden beam overhead. With a final push to send her swinging, Jake jumped back out of the way.

As the chains unraveled, Margie let out a whoop of delight. When the tire finally swung to a stop, Margie let herself fall backward onto the ground, laughing at her dizziness.

When she felt steady enough to stand, she pulled herself to her feet, giving Jake another opportunity to laugh at her as she stumbled about. "Okay, wise guy, you try it," she challenged him.

With ease, he scrambled on top the tire and braced his elbows around the chains. "Go for it."

Grabbing the chains, Margie began spinning the tire and the smiling Jake in circles. When she could take it no more, she backed away and watched the tire slow, then begin to pick up speed going the opposite direction as the chains untwisted. She reached out and pushed the tire to give it extra back and forth motion.

Jake squealed with delight. When the tire stopped moving, he begged, "Do it again!"

Margie smiled and complied happily.

After his third turn, Margie was rescued from another spin by Mrs. Grafton's approach. "I brought you something to snack on. Looks like you're working up an appetite out here." She was positively beaming.

"Thanks," Margie said, taking the offered lemonade.

Jake clambered off the swing and chugged back his lemonade without taking a breath. "Thanks, Grammy," he said when he finished.

She laughed. "I'll bring some more. Have some cookies." Mrs. Grafton set the tray in the grass and headed back to the house.

Margie took a cookie and sat on the bottom of the slide. "These are great!" she said.

"They aren't as good as my mom's," Jake said.

Margie could see his mood change in an instant. "It's hard when they're gone, isn't it?"

He shrugged.

"The first time my dad left, I wouldn't come out of my room for a week," Margie shared.

Jake looked at her, but she stared off into the distance.

She went on. "I'm really proud of him. He works on the planes your mom flies."

"Really?"

"Yep. He's there to keep her safe."

Margie heard the boy sniffle. "Why'd she have to go?"

"There are bad people in the world, hurting other people." Margie heard her dad's words coming from her mouth. "They need someone to protect them, and to help them repair their country."

"My mom doesn't protect people," Jake mumbled.

"Sure she does! Can you hear when a plane flies by?" she asked.

Jake nodded.

"Well, so can the bad guys, and they get scared. They know the American planes and the pilots are the best in the world, so they have to hide. When they're hiding, they can't hurt people." Margie thought that was the best way to explain war to an eight-year-old. She knew there was more to it, and had watched the news with her parents often enough to know planes can cause a lot of destruction.

Jake seemed to accept that explanation. He looked at Margie with newfound interest. "Want to play catch?" he asked.

Chapter 11

The River Creek tournament was going well for the Lady Tigers. On Saturday, they had won the first two games, and only lost the third by one run.

It was a beautiful Sunday morning, the skies filled with large, fluffy white clouds. The air was still cool, so the girls wore their warm-up jackets over their uniforms as they tossed the ball back and forth.

"Margie! Hey, Margie!"

Margie and her friends turned at the sound of the voice and saw a gaggle of children pressed up against the fence, jumping up and down and waving. The girls laughed and waved back.

The kids from the skills clinic continued to call out to various girls, trying to outdo each other.

"Well, go see your fans and get it over with," Coach Kory said cheerfully.

The girls jogged to the fence and greeted the young children.

"I came to watch you play," one seven-year-old girl told Tammy.

"And I'm so glad you did!" Tammy returned. "We'll play even better with this crowd cheering for us."

The kids talked excitedly for a few more minutes before the coaches called the Tigers back to their warm-ups.

Shortly, the coin toss and rule reminders were over, and the game began. Amy led off. "C'mon, Amy!" the kids yelled. The sound of their young voices made her smile as she stepped into the box.

She watched the first pitch go by. The second pitch was low and outside, perfect for the bunt she expertly laid down the first base line. She flew toward first base and beat the throw by a step.

The children roared with excitement.

Sally batted next. The first pitch was a ball that she let go by. The next pitch was pretty, and she stepped as if to hit it, but then stopped herself at the last minute.

"Strike!" the umpire declared.

But by then, Amy was already well on her way to second base on a steal. The catcher jumped up, threw the ball accurately, but Amy easily slid in before the tag. The kids on the sidelines screamed in delight.

The next good pitch that came close to the plate, Sally sent flying up the middle into centerfield. Amy was off with the pitch, rounding third as the centerfielder picked it up, trying to decide where to throw the ball. Amy stood her ground, waiting on the decision.

Finally, the outfielder threw the ball to the pitcher and Amy went back to third. Sally remained on first base.

Tammy stepped into the batter's box. On the first pitch, Sally jogged toward second base, trying to draw the throw from the catcher. The opposing team didn't take the bait, and let her reach second safely.

On the second pitch, Tammy squared in the box, trying to bunt the ball, but fouled it off instead. Now she had two strikes against her. The next two pitches were balls; the count was two and two.

As the next pitch came in, Tammy squared at the last minute, bunting the ball toward third base, halfway between the pitcher and the third baseman. Bunting on two strikes was tricky, because if the ball had gone foul again, she would have been out. This worked to her advantage, as the fielders didn't expect it and had been playing deep, away from home plate.

As the defense rushed to field the ball, Amy's speed allowed her to cross the plate. The third baseman hurried to throw the ball to first base to get Tammy out, but in her haste, overthrew the first baseman and sent the ball flying past her into the fence. Sally rounded third and easily made it home as Tammy raced to second base.

The Tigers' crowd cheered as the ball was thrown back to the pitcher and the fielders set themselves again.

Trish stepped to the plate.

"Don't leave me out here, Trish!" Tammy called from second base.

Stealing a glance backward at the catcher, Trish looked to see where she was set up. The catcher squatted behind the plate on the outside corner. As the pitcher entered her windup, Trish inched closer to the plate.

The ball crossed the plate high and outside, but Trish extended her arms and connected with the ball, sending it into right-center field.

Tammy raced to third and rounded to watch for the throw. Trish hit first base and started toward second. The right fielder picked up the ball. Seeing Trish's movement, she threw the ball to second base. The fielder caught the throw and swept her arm down for the tag, but caught only air. Trish had drawn the throw, then stopped, ready to retreat to first base if necessary.

Immediately upon the throw to second, Tammy had made a dash toward home plate. Seeing that the runner from first was not moving, the second baseman whipped the ball toward home plate in an effort to stop the run. Too late. Tammy had crossed the plate and now Trish arrived safely at second base.

The kids howled and cheered on the sideline. The parents were on their feet clapping as Tammy did her happy dance on the way back to the dugout.

Trish stood on second base, grinning ear-to-ear as the coach from the other team called a time out to talk to his girls.

An hour later, the game ended, the Lady Tigers winning 5 to 1.

The girls cleaned out the dugout and moved under a shade tree to await their next game. Two more teams from the tournament took their places on the field and another game was underway. The kids from the clinic gathered around and peppered the Tigers with questions.

"How do you know when to run or not?" one boy asked.

"Sometimes the coaches tell us. That's why they stand out there," Margie pointed at the coaches standing next to the first and third base bags. "Sometimes we have to decide by ourselves if we think we can make it. That means we have to pay attention to where the ball is, what the fielders are doing, and where the other runners are."

"Wow! That's a lot to know at the same time," a six-year old said with awe.

"The more you play, the easier it gets," Amy explained.

"That's why we do so many drills," Margie explained. "The same ones we're teaching you."

"Those were just games," someone commented.

Margie and Amy shook their heads. "They're fun, but they are meant to teach you something you'll need later when you're playing ball," Margie said.

"Can we play again?" That question was echoed with excited cries from the other kids as they jumped up and down.

The other Tigers that were resting nearby laughed. "Hey, Margie, you have fans!" Trish said.

"You've created some softball and baseball lovers," Amy added.

Margie smiled broadly. She noticed Jake stood on the outside of the group. He wasn't cheering, but he also wasn't scowling. Margie felt that was improvement.

Chapter 12

The next morning, Margie woke up excited to call her dad. She knew it was too early and that he would still be at work. She had to try to time her phone call so it was after he got off work, but before he went to bed.

"Margie, will you please stop fidgeting?" her mom said with a smile in her voice. "What has gotten into you?"

"I have an idea about the next clinic, but I have to ask Dad something."

"Why don't you text him and ask him to call you?"

Margie palmed her forehead. She hadn't thought of that on her own, but she should have. Quickly, she sent her dad a message. Then she waited.

Just as she, Tara, and her mother were sitting down for lunch, her cell phone rang.

"Dad! I'm so glad you called!" Margie said as soon as she pushed the talk button on her phone.

"Sorry I couldn't get back to you sooner. I was in an area where I couldn't have my phone with me so I just now got your text."

"That's okay. Hey, I have an idea." Margie rambled for ten minutes, not giving her dad a chance to get a word in.

When she finally paused for breath, she could hear him chuckling 8,000 miles away. "I think that could work. Let me see what we have on this end to set it up. I'll let you know. When do you want to do this?"

"In two weeks?" she said in more of a question than a statement. "Is that too soon?"

"No, actually I think that would work out well. I'll look at the flying schedule and get back to you. Think I could talk to your mom for a bit?"

"Sure! Love you, Dad!" Margie handed the phone to her mother and took over keeping Tara entertained while her mom walked into the living room to talk to her husband in private.

"Did you hear that, Tara?" Margie asked her little sister. "We're going to be on TV!"

"TV!" Tara repeated, tossing her arms in the air, sprinkling Cheerios with the motion.

Chapter 13

Two weeks went by quickly as Margie and her friends made all the preparations. The whole team pitched in this time to make posters, pass out flyers, and make phone calls to parents from her dad's unit. It was time to put her plan into action. Thankfully it was a beautiful, sunny day. It had rained the night before, making it hard for Margie to sleep because she was worried it would ruin her plans.

Now her teammates were arriving at the field and getting right to work setting up their stations. They knew the drills by now, and Margie didn't have to tell them what needed to be done.

"Margie, there's someone I'd like you to meet," Coach Kory said, gesturing her over to the bleachers.

Margie jogged over.

"Margie, this is Mr. Adkins. I told him about your idea and he would like to help."

Margie shook his offered hand. "We can use all the help we can get, sir. Thanks for being here."

Even to her own ears, she sounded so grown up that she knew her dad would be proud.

"Margie, I own my own audiovisual company in town. I brought some equipment that I thought would make your task a little easier." Mr. Adkins waved over a few men that were hauling equipment from a van nearby. "These men will be your camera crew. You can tell them where you want them to be to film. You get to call the shots."

"Really?" Margie said. "That's awesome! I can't thank you enough." Inside, Margie's mind was reeling. This was even better than she had hoped. She had planned on using cell phones to transmit video of the kids.

Just then her phone rang. "Excuse me," she said to the two men. She stepped away to answer the call from her dad.

"Hi, Pumpkin," he said. "Are you ready to test this?"

Margie started to explain about Mr. Adkins.

"I know. Your mom told me and we're all set up on this end."

"Really? Why didn't anyone tell me?"

"We didn't want to disappoint you if it didn't work out. Why don't you put Mr. Adkins on the line and we'll get this party started?"

Margie laughed. It was funny to hear her dad talk like that. She handed the phone to Mr. Adkins. "It's for you."

She went back onto the field to tell the girls the great news.

As the kids starting arriving for the clinic, they gawked at the camera equipment and the awning that was set up behind the backstop with the large movie screen. Margie was pleased to see Jake arrive with his father.

"What's going on?" Jake asked her.

"We're going to do something a little special today," she explained.

When she wouldn't tell him anything more, he ran onto the field with the other kids, seemingly happy to be here.

"Thanks for taking extra time with him," Jake's father said to Margie after Jake had gone. "He's taking the separation from his mother pretty hard."

"I remember the first time my father left. It wasn't easy," she admitted.

"Jake's been looking forward to today," Mr. Grafton said, "although his grandma slipped once and called it a softball clinic. That got him going." He laughed at the memory.

Margie laughed with him. "Well, he's a good player. He's just a little hesitant at taking advice from a girl."

"Well, I think you'll see a change in him after watching you girls play a few weeks ago. All he could talk about was how far you all could hit the ball."

"I better get going," she said. "Thanks for bringing him."

"Wouldn't miss it for the world," he said.

Margie joined her team as the kids practiced throwing.

"Why are those men here?" one little girl asked.

"Are we making a movie?" another boy added.

Margie smile. "Not exactly. But we do have a special surprise for you. Be good and listen to everything we tell you."

The kids focused on making good throws and catches. Finally, Margie called them into the shade under the awning. She had all the kids sit on the ground facing the screen.

"There are some folks that want to see you," she said, stepping aside as the projector came on and revealed a room filled with smiling faces of people wearing desert camouflage uniforms.

The kids squealed with delight and started waving excitedly. The parents on the other end of the camera waved back.

She noticed Jake was straining his neck, searching the screen. From the look on his face, she could tell that he was unable to spot his mother.

After a few moments, Margie called to get the kids' attention. "Okay, okay." She smiled. "You'll all get your chance to talk to your parents, but for now, they're waiting to see you play ball. Want to show them what you've learned?"

"Yeah!" they all yelled, barely able to contain their excitement. Jake sat still, not responding.

"Then let's call it off," she said, motioning them into a circle around her. All the kids put their right hand into the circle, just like they were taught. Margie leaned in and whispered something only for their ears. They smiled back at her and nodded their heads, except for Jake, who went through the motions without enthusiasm.

"On the count of three," she said. "One, two, three…"

The kids threw their hands in the air as one and yelled, "Air Force!"

The parents gathered in a building somewhere in Afghanistan clapped their approval and waved as the kids ran to take their place on the field.

Margie divided the kids into stations and sent them to work. Mr. Adkins' cameramen followed the kids onto the field and took turns moving from station to station, filming the action.

From the back of his open van, Mr. Adkins sat behind a control board that pushed the camera feeds to a large screen at the Air Force base. He was good at ensuring that each child got equal screen time.

Chapter 14

Margie approached Jake as he stood waiting his turn at the soft toss station. She kneeled beside him and picked at the grass. "You don't look very happy to be here," she offered.

He shrugged.

"Remember we talked about the important job our parents have?"

He shrugged again.

"Your mom would be here if she could," Margie said.

"It's Saturday," Jake said, as if that explained everything.

"Bad guys don't take the weekend off," Margie explained. "Our parents have to work every day when they're gone."

"Those parents aren't working," he accused.

"I'm sure they're coming off work or are on their way. My dad said they tried to work the schedule to get as many people free during this time as possible."

"Hey, Jake," his father called from the fence. "Come here a minute."

Jake jogged over to meet his father by the awning.

"There's someone here that wants to see you," he said, motioning for Jake to go into the shade.

Jake grinned broadly, happy to see his mother on the big screen.

"Sorry I was late, Jake. I got here as fast as I could. I had a sortie to fly." Jake knew that meant she had been flying her jet. She was still dressed in her flight suit, and he could see that her hair was wet and matted from sweating under the helmet.

"Have you been watching us play?" he asked.

"I see you moping around mostly," Captain Grafton said. "The girls went to a lot of trouble to make this a good day for you. You need to enjoy it."

"Want to see me hit?" he asked, dismissing her scolding.

"Of course! Go for it! I'm watching."

Jake shoved a helmet onto his head, joined the line inside the dugout, and waited for his turn to bat. He was called to the plate next.

"Remember, eye on the ball," Coach Dave said as Jake took his place.

When Jake nodded, Coach Dave threw the baseball to the catcher. Jake swung, connecting with the ball on the first try. It sailed into the outfield where three younger players converged to scoop it up.

Jake dropped his bat and ran back to the screen under the awning, where his mother's face was still prominent. "Did you see that?" he asked excitedly.

"I sure did!" she said with a big grin. "But I think you're supposed to run to first base, not off the field!"

Chapter 15

Throughout the afternoon, Mr. Adkins rotated the kids through a station he set up under the awning so they could talk to their parents one-on-one. On the big screen, he continued the loop from station to station so the parents could see their children play.

Margie noted that the kids were on their best behavior, focusing intently on the directions given to them by the Lady Tiger players. They were out to make a good impression, and it showed.

Jake especially was all smiles. Margie watched him zip through the stations multiple times. When the camera was on him, he waved enthusiastically at his mother on the other end. He couldn't see her from the field, but knowing she was on the other side of that link made his day extra special.

When Margie finally called them all into the awning for the final cheer, she was pleasantly surprised to see the parents on the screen also gather into a circle. The kids put their right hands into their circle and, on the count of three, cheered, "Air Force!"

They turned their attention to the screen where the parents were doing their own countdown. Hands thrown into the air, they cheered, "Tigers!"

As the parents gathered their children to take home, Jake found Margie talking with Trish and Tammy. Unexpectedly, he threw his arms around her waist and squeezed.

Taken off guard, Margie laughed and hugged him back. "What's that for?" she asked.

"Thanks for bringing my mom to me," he answered. He released her and stepped back. "She wants me to teach her how to hit better when she gets back. She says I hit farther than she does!" The pride in his voice was measurable.

"That's great!" Tammy said. "You better keep practicing."

"Oh, I will," he replied. "Dad said he's going to get some stuff from the store so we can set up stations in our backyard like you did here.

"You know, Mom said what she's doing over there is really important," Jake said.

Margie nodded. "Just like we talked about, right?"

"Yep. But she also said what you are doing here is really important too."

Margie was surprised. "What did she mean?"

"She said you are taking care of us so she and the other parents there can take care of those people."

"I guess that's true," Margie said. "We just wanted to do something fun for you guys."

"It was a lot of fun!" Jake said. "Are you going to do it again?"

Tammy and Trish, who had been following this exchange, groaned playfully.

Margie smiled at Jake. "No, I think we are done for this year. We have to practice for our own team," she explained.

Jake hung his head.

"But I think your dad might have some good news for you on that front," she added quickly.

He raised his eyes to meet hers.

She gestured toward Mr. Grafton, who was talking to the three Lady Tigers' coaches near the bleachers. "Go ask him," she suggested.

Jake took a few steps toward his dad, then stopped and ran back to Margie. Giving her one more quick squeeze, he raced away without another word.

"What's going on?" Tammy asked.

"Jake's dad is going to start a team from the base," Margie said. "It's going to be coach-pitch. At that age, girls and boys play on the same team anyway, so he thinks he'll be able to keep most of the kids from the unit together—as long as they are in the right age range."

"I'll bet he'll be able to get more parents to help at the other age levels," Trish put in. "They all seemed really interested in what we were doing here."

Margie nodded. "It'll be a great distraction for the kids while they wait for the deployment to be over."

"Thanks for putting this together, Margie," Tammy said.

"Why are you thanking me? You all pitched in. I couldn't have done it without you."

"Yeah, but you got it going. And it was a lot of fun for us too," Trish said.

"My parents aren't military so I can't imagine how I'd feel if one of them had to leave for a long time," Tammy said.

"I guess that's why it's good to do stuff like this," Margie said. "Gives us a chance to see things from a different viewpoint."

"Margie," Coach Dave called. "Your dad wants to talk to you before Mr. Adkins closes up shop."

Margie jogged to where the awning was still in place, although most of the equipment had been removed. The big screen was down so she sat in front of the laptop that was open on a table. Her father's smiling face greeted her.

"Great job, Pumpkin!" he said. "You sure made our day. Heck, our week! They'll be talking about this the rest of the deployment."

"The kids were pretty excited too," Margie shared. "I think they got the message that their parents still care, even when they have to be gone."

"And that people at home care, too." her father added. "You and your team didn't have to take up your Saturdays doing this for them. I think it shows a lot of compassion that you helped them to connect with their parents from such a distance."

"It was a team effort," Margie said, smiling at her pun. "The Lady Tigers really pulled together for this. And we gained a whole new crowd of fans!"

"Well, I have to get back to work," her dad said. "Give your mom and your sister a kiss from me."

Margie blew her dad a kiss and he caught it over the video feed.

"You sure had a great turnout at the clinic," Coach Kory said to Margie as they were putting away all the equipment.

"It's a lot of work," Margie said. "I don't know how you do it for us a couple days a week."

The coach thought about his words as he folded up the netting they used for soft toss. "How did it feel when one of the kids you were helping finally got it right?" he asked.

"Awesome!" Margie answered without hesitation.

Coach Kory smiled at her. "That's why we do it."

#######

Get to Know the Game

Fastpitch softball: The ball is pitched underhand with no arc, and typically with speed. The speed varies depending on the age, skill of the pitcher, and type of pitch thrown.

Infield: A dirt square with a base in each corner. The distance between bases changes depending on the age of the players. Sometimes baseball has grass on the infield for older players.

Outfield: The grassy area behind the infield that stops (usually) at a fence.

Field: The place where softball (or baseball) is played. Typically a dirt infield with a grassy outfield.

Diamond: This refers to the infield, plus the dirt around it all the way to the grass. Because the infield is positioned so the batter stands at one of its corners, it is called a diamond rather than a square.

Home plate: A five-sided, flat piece of rubber set level with the ground. The pitcher throws the ball toward the plate so the batter can hit.

Rubber or Mound: The place where the pitcher stands to pitch the ball toward home plate.

Pitcher's circle: A circle drawn in a wide area around the pitcher's rubber.

Batter's box: A rectangle drawn on either side of the plate in chalk that is large enough for the batter to stand (right- or left-handed). The batter is allowed to stand anywhere within the box, but must be in the box when hitting the ball.

Umpire: The person that stands behind the catcher at home plate. The umpire calls balls and strikes, and ensures that everyone is following the rules of the game.

Runner: A batter that has made it to a base without getting out.

Lead off: In fastpitch softball, the runner cannot leave the base until the ball leaves the pitcher's hand. That gives them a slight head start when the ball is hit. Just because they take a lead, it does not mean they are required to run to the next base. But the runner can be tagged out if a fielder touches them with the ball when they are not touching the base.

Steal: If the runner chooses to run to the next base when the ball has not been hit, it is a steal. They take the risk of being tagged out so it doesn't happen every time.

Foul ball: A ball hit by the batter that does not stay within the boundaries drawn in chalk starting from home plate, straight over first base and out to the fence. Another line is drawn from home plate over third base and out to the fence. A "fair ball" must be inside those lines when it hits the ground.

Strikes: A ball pitched over the plate between the knees and armpits of the batter. It also refers to when a batter swings and misses the ball. A foul ball is also a strike.

Ball: In reference to balls and strikes, a ball is when the pitch is not over the plate, or is lower than the batter's knees, or is higher than the batter's armpits.

Strike out: A batter gets three strikes, and then she or he is out and it is the next person's turn to bat. Foul balls are counted differently. In most cases, a foul ball on the third strike does not count and the batter can continue to try until the ball is hit fair or a third strike is called.

Change-up: A pitch that is thrown much slower than the fastpitch. It is meant to catch batters off guard and cause them to swing early and miss.

Bunt: Instead of swinging at the pitch, the batter turns to face the pitcher and puts the bat across the plate. In this way, the ball hits the bat and doesn't travel as far, usually stopping somewhere between the catcher and the pitcher.

Fly ball: A ball hit into the air with an arc.

Line drive: A hard hit ball that has no arc.

Positions: The places on the field where the players stand. The exact location will change depending on the play, where the runners are on the field, and what the defense thinks the batter is going to do. In addition to the title of the position, the positions are also assigned position numbers that the scorekeeper uses to track the game. See the numbers next to the positions below.

1. **Pitcher**: The person that stands on the pitcher's mound and throws the ball over the plate. The pitcher's goal is to strike the batter out. For softball, the ball must be pitched underhand. For baseball, it is thrown overhand.

2. **Catcher**: The player that squats behind home plate to receive the pitch. Because they are so close to the batter, the catcher must wear a helmet, mask, chest protector, and shin guards. Sometimes the catcher will also have a special glove that has extra padding. This is called a catcher's mitt.

3. **First baseman**: To the catcher's right, there is a bag (usually white) a certain distance down the foul line. The first baseman stands with the bag about four feet to her left.

4. **Second baseman**: Stands halfway between the first base bag and the second base bag. The second base bag is opposite home plate on the field.

5. **Third baseman**: To the catcher's left, there is a bag (usually white) a certain distance down the foul line.

The third baseman stands with the bag about four feet to their right.

6. **Shortstop**: Stands halfway between the second base bag and the third base bag.

7. **Left field**: In the grass behind the shortstop.

8. **Centerfield**: In the grass behind the second base bag.

9. **Right field**: In the grass behind the second baseman.

Line-up: The order in which the batters hit. It can be in any order the coach decides, but the batters must remain in the same order throughout that game. A player can be replaced during a game, in which case the new batter must bat in the spot the person replaced was batting.

Out: Each team gets three outs per inning. An out can be made in many ways: striking out, tagging a base runner when she is not touching the base, catching a hit ball before it touches the ground, and throwing a hit ball to a base ahead of the runner when the runner is required to move. There are others, but this covers the most common examples.

Inning: When each team has had three outs the inning is over. The "top of the inning" is when the first team to bat is batting. The "bottom of the inning" is when the team that fielded first is batting. Softball is played for seven innings, unless there is a tie; then the game may go longer. Baseball typically plays nine innings.

Time limit: Often in tournament settings, a time limit is set on a game. It may be an hour and fifteen minutes or seven innings, whichever comes first. The time limit is set by the tournament director and can vary on different days or different tournaments. This helps keep the tournament on schedule.

Home team: The team that is in the field (defense) first at the beginning of the game.

Visitors: The team that bats (offensive) first at the beginning of the game.

Discussion Questions

1. Why was Margie mad at her father?

2. If one of your parents had to go away for a long time, how would that make you feel?

3. What did the Lady Tigers do to help Margie when she was sad about her father being gone?

4. Can you think of other ways the Lady Tigers might have helped the kids from the squadron?

5. What lesson was Margie trying to teach Jake?

6. Who was your favorite character and why?

About the Author

Dawn Brotherton started playing fastpitch when she was nine years old. Throughout the years she has played travel ball, coached, umpired, and kept score. Now she's writing about it! Her Lady Tigers' series is written to encourage reading, sports, and friendship to young readers.

She is the author of six books, including the Lady Tigers Series and the Jackie Austin Mystery Series. Dawn is also a contributing author to *A-10s Over Kosovo*, a compilation of stories about being deployed for Operation ALLIED FORCE. Dawn has been awarded a Global Ebook Bronze Award for her writing.

She recently retired as a colonel in the United States Air Force and has settled with her family in Williamsburg, Virginia, where she is hard at work on more Lady Tigers' adventures.

From the Author

I hope you enjoyed reading about Margie and her friends. There is more to come and more people to meet. If you have ideas you want to share with me or softball questions to ask, please get in touch with me at <u>Dawn@DawnBrothertonAuthor.com</u>. I'd love to hear from you.
To learn more about the Tigers, check out <u>LadyTigersFastpich.com</u>.

Other books by Dawn Brotherton:
Lady Tigers' Series

Trish's Team
Margie Makes a Difference
Nicole's New Friend (coming soon)

Softball Scoresheet

CPSIA information can be obtained
at www.ICGtesting.com
Printed in the USA
FFOW03n1042020418
46106095-47121FF